A GIFT FOR:

_____

FROM:

_____

Story time and play time are a lot more fun when You're The Star!

Story time

1. Put on the cape and secure it around your shoulders.
2. Turn the medallion to ON using the switch located on its side.
3. Press the front of the medallion one time to begin story time!

- *When an adult reads the highlighted phrases in the book, you'll hear music, voices, and other sounds.*

Play time

1. Put on the cape and secure it around your shoulders.
2. Turn the medallion to ON using the switch located on its side.
3. Press the front of the medallion two times to begin play time!

- *Say the trigger phrases listed in the back of each book to hear more sounds and to make play time even more fun!*

Collect all of Princess Harmony's books to find out more magical phrases!

Editorial Director: Carrie Bolin
Editor: Nate Barbarick
Art Director: Jan Mastin
Designer: Brian Pilachowski
Production Designer: Bryan Ring
Colorist: Cathy McQuitty-Dreiling
Colorist: Lynda Calvert-Weyant

ISBN: 978-1-59530-934-1
K0B8095
Printed and bound in China
OCT13

PRINCESS
HARMONY™
AND THE OVERNIGHT CAMPOUT

BY MEGAN HAAVE

ILLUSTRATED BY KARLA TAYLOR

Hallmark

Princess Harmony could hardly wait for her very first campout. As Queen Nana helped her pack, she asked her, "What are you most looking forward to tonight?"

"Hmm, it's hard to choose," said Harmony. "A warm campfire, yummy treats . . . but I'd say all the friends to have fun with!"

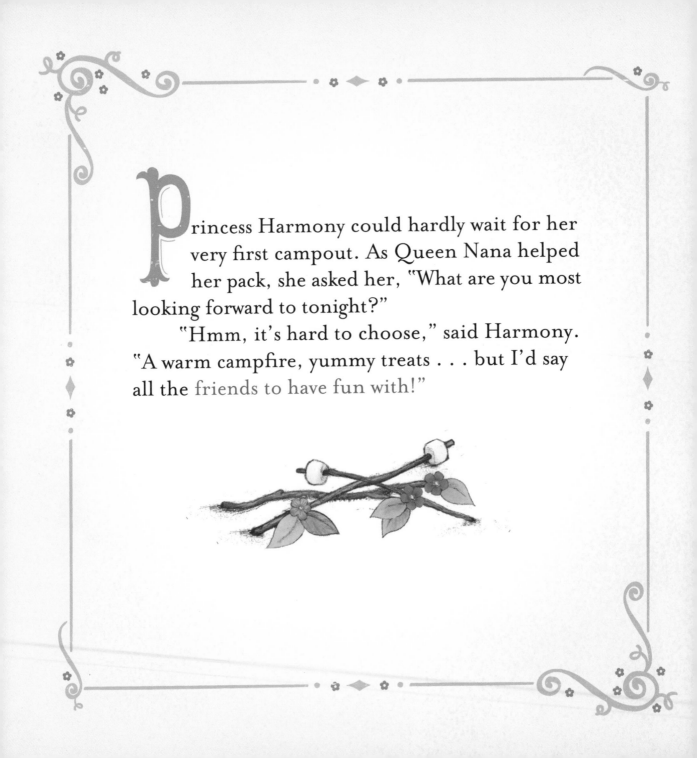

Everyone was eager to set up camp. But Harmony soon learned that that her friends, being animals, didn't know the first thing about camping.

"Where's the door on this thing?" grumbled Hip.

"These flowers will make our fire smell lovely!" said Simon.

"Thanks for all your help," said Harmony. "Preparing a campsite can be tricky, but it will be easier if we work together. Follow me and I'll show you."

Alice raised the tent, while Hip and Hop
staked it to the ground. Patty, Henry, and Simon
finally got the campfire going.

After a job well done, it was time to eat. " . . . Next, you make a little sandwich," Harmony explained. "Then, take a bite!"

"Mmmph mmm mmmrgh!" mumbled Simon.

"Simon says he likes the s'mores," noted Henry.

Harmony giggled, glad to see everyone's happy faces. The campfire was good, the s'mores were even better, but Harmony thought her friends were the best.

The campers felt full and happy, so happy that they wanted to play music. So they played and played, until the day became twilight.

"I could do this all night!" boasted Henry. The other animals agreed.

"*Not me,*" thought Harmony, who began to miss her comfy bed in the castle. Just as she imagined resting her head on her pillow, her friends began to play a little ditty.

"So much for sleeping," sighed Harmony, trudging to the tent. "Maybe changing into pajamas will remind everyone that it's almost bedtime." When she dug into her bag, she felt something strange.

My Dear Harmony,

Let this bracelet remind you that love goes with you everywhere. When you wear it, I hope you feel how special you are to your family and friends.

Love and Hugs,
Nana

Instantly, Harmony felt better. Although she was too sleepy to really enjoy the music, the bracelet reminded her of how much she loved being with her friends. Watching them play around the campfire, Harmony was filled with gratitude.

Sleepiness began to get the best of the animals.
"Sheesh!" yelled Hop. "Am I the only one
around here who thinks this music sounds terrible?"
"I wouldn't say terrible," answered Harmony,
"but a lullaby might be more of a crowd-pleaser.
Play along with me!"
Her friends joined her as she sang:
*"When the stars and the moon light the night sky above,
it's so nice to be next to the ones who you love."*

Harmony soon noticed that Patty looked sad. "Patty," she asked, "what's wrong?"

"I want to go home," she said. "I'm not feeling so good, and I just remembered how nice and soft my bed is."

"Patty, wait here for just a minute," said Harmony,
dashing off into the forest. "I have an idea!"
"Isn't *anyone* staying?" sighed Hop.
The animals weren't so sure about this.

After a while, the animals couldn't wait anymore. They started circling the campsite, looking for their princess. "Princess?" they shouted, to the stillness of the woods.

Soon, they saw a shadow near a rustling bush, and to their surprise, it was Harmony, holding flowers.

"Whew!" said Simon. "I was starting to worry, Princess!"

"Oh, Harmony," added Alice, "we're so glad we found you."

The animals gathered to see what was in her hand. "Patty, I know you're feeling a little homesick, so I made you this bracelet to remind you that love goes with you everywhere. Please stay at the campout . . . it wouldn't be the same if you left."

Patty smiled. "Wow, Princess. I love it! Yes, my bed at home is nice and soft, but all my friends will be here. I think I'll stay!" Surrounded by her pals, Patty was filled with gratitude.

When the fire was out, the friends snuggled up to sleep. As they said their good nights, Patty remembered a line from Harmony's lullaby. "It's so nice to be next to the ones who you love," she said.

"It really is, Patty," replied Harmony, as her eyes grew heavy and closed.

Patty then slid her flute from underneath the blanket and stood up. She blew a loud note, stirring up the other animals. "And you know what else, Princess Harmony? It sure is fun to play together!"

Turn the page for more fun with Princess Harmony!

Press the medallion one more time,
then try saying these phrases
when you're out playing!

I'm the Princess!

Oh, fiddlesticks!

Play my song!

I love you!

Let's have a ball!

Time to dance!

Charmed, I'm sure!

Maybe I can help!

⸙⁓⁓ NEW ⁓⁓⸙

Look what I can do!

Discover even more fun phrases in other Princess Harmony books!

If you have enjoyed
Princess Harmony's adventure,
we would love to hear from you.

Please send your comments to:

Hallmark Book Feedback

P.O. Box 419034

Mail Drop 100

Kansas City, MO 64141

Or e-mail us at:

booknotes@hallmark.com